Say Hello to the Jungle Animals!

Ian Whybrow   Ed Eaves

Say Hello to the Jungle Animals!

MACMILLAN CHILDREN'S BOOKS

Through the jungle – off we go!
Come along and say hello.

A wrinkly rhino's eating lunch.
Plenty of reeds for him to munch.

Hello, Rhino!

Crunch,

crunch,

crunch!

Even the hungry crocodile
Has the time to stop and smile.

Hello, Crocodile!

Snap!

Snap!

Snap!

Like a shadow through the trees
A panther wanders at his ease.

Watch this cobra shiver and shake.
Say hello to the dancing snake!

Hello, Snake!

Sssssss, ssssss, sssssss!

Let's all creep on tippy-toe.
There's a tiger down below!

Hello, sleeping Tiger!
Prrrrr, prrrrr, prrrrr!

I see bats in the evening sky
Call hello as they fly by.

Hello, Bats!

Eeeek! Eeeek!
Eeeek!

Now let's leave the jungle path.
The river's just right for a cooling bath!

Hello, Mummy Elephant!
Swish, swosh, swish!

Let's come out to sit and dry.
Can you wave and say goodbye?

Goodbye, Rhino!

Crunch, crunch, crunch!

Goodbye, Crocodile!

Snap! Snap! Snap!

Goodbye, Panther!

Pad-pad-pad!

Goodbye, Snake!

Sssssss, sssssss, sssssss!

Goodbye, Tiger!
Prrrrr, prrrrr, prrrrr!

Goodbye, Bats!
Eeeek! Eeeek! Eeeek!

Goodbye, Elephants!
Swish, swosh, swish!

If you'd like to look once more,
Follow me and let's explore!

For Fifi and Amelie with love – I.W.

For Ysella – E.E.

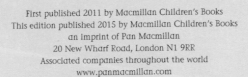

First published 2011 by Macmillan Children's Books
This edition published 2015 by Macmillan Children's Books
an imprint of Pan Macmillan
20 New Wharf Road, London N1 9RR
Associated companies throughout the world
www.panmacmillan.com

ISBN: 978-1-5098-0137-4

Text copyright © Ian Whybrow 2011
Illustrations copyright © Ed Eaves 2011
Moral rights asserted.

1 3 5 7 9 8 6 4 2

A CIP catalogue record for this book is available from the British Library.

Printed in China